Who is My Best Friend?

By: Summer Amaya

ISBN 978-1-7361999-6-1

Library of Congress Catalog Card Number 2021906023

Who is My Best Friend?

Written by: Summer Amaya

Cover Design: Rumana Rupa

Printed in the United States of America

I would like to dedicate this book to Mrs. Michelle Obama. In school, I learned that Mrs. Michelle Obama wrote an autobiography that inspired me to write a book about something that truly happened to me. Thank you! Summer Amaya

Ashely and Vanessa were best friends since kindergarten. They went to Jackson Elementary School.

They always played at school and sat next to each other in the lunchroom.

On the first day of school, as first graders, Ashely and Vanessa were so excited to see each other.

They talked about everything they had done while on vacation. Ashley went to basketball camp, and Vanessa went to dance school.

As Mrs. Smith started class, she asked the class to open their notebooks for Science.

Principal Johnson opens the classroom door and introduces a new student named Jennifer Hill.

Mrs. Smith tells Jennifer to sit in the empty seat next to Ashley.

As Jennifer sits next to Ashley, she says, "Hi, my name is Jennifer. What is your name?"

Ashley smiled and said, "My name is Ashley; nice to meet you." The two girls worked together in science class and had fun.

After Science, the class goes to the lunchroom. Ashley asks Jennifer to come and sit with her and Vanessa.

The two girls walked over to Vanessa's table to sit down. When Vanessa sees Ashley and Jennifer, she became confused and angry.

Vanessa asks Ashley, "Why would you be friends with the new girl?" Ashley says, "Because she is nice and doesn't know anyone in the school."

Vanessa tells Ashley she doesn't want to be friends with the new girl. Ashley responds by saying, "We were both the new girl last year and became the best of friends."

"Why can't you be nice? If you get to know Jennifer, you will see she is really nice," Ashley suggested.

"You can be friends with whoever you want to be friends with," Vanessa states.

Ashley and Jennifer moved and sat at another table.

As Ashley and Jennifer were enjoying their lunch, Vanessa walked to their table. She said to both Ashley and Jennifer, "I'm sorry for being mean. I became jealous and thought that you were trying to take my friend away, Jennifer."

Ashley said, "If you want to be my friend, you will need to be friendlier to others. It is okay to have more than one friend Vanessa."

Jennifer says to Vanessa, "It's okay. We can start over and be friends."

Vanessa asked Ashely and Jennifer if she could sit with them at lunch. The girls said at the same time, "Yes, you can sit with us." Vanessa was happy, and the girls started to talk about their favorite hobbies.

Jennifer told the girls that she loved ballet and wanted to be a famous dancer when she grows up! From there, Vanessa realized how much she had in common with Jennifer. Vanessa couldn't believe that Jennifer loved ballet just as much as she did!

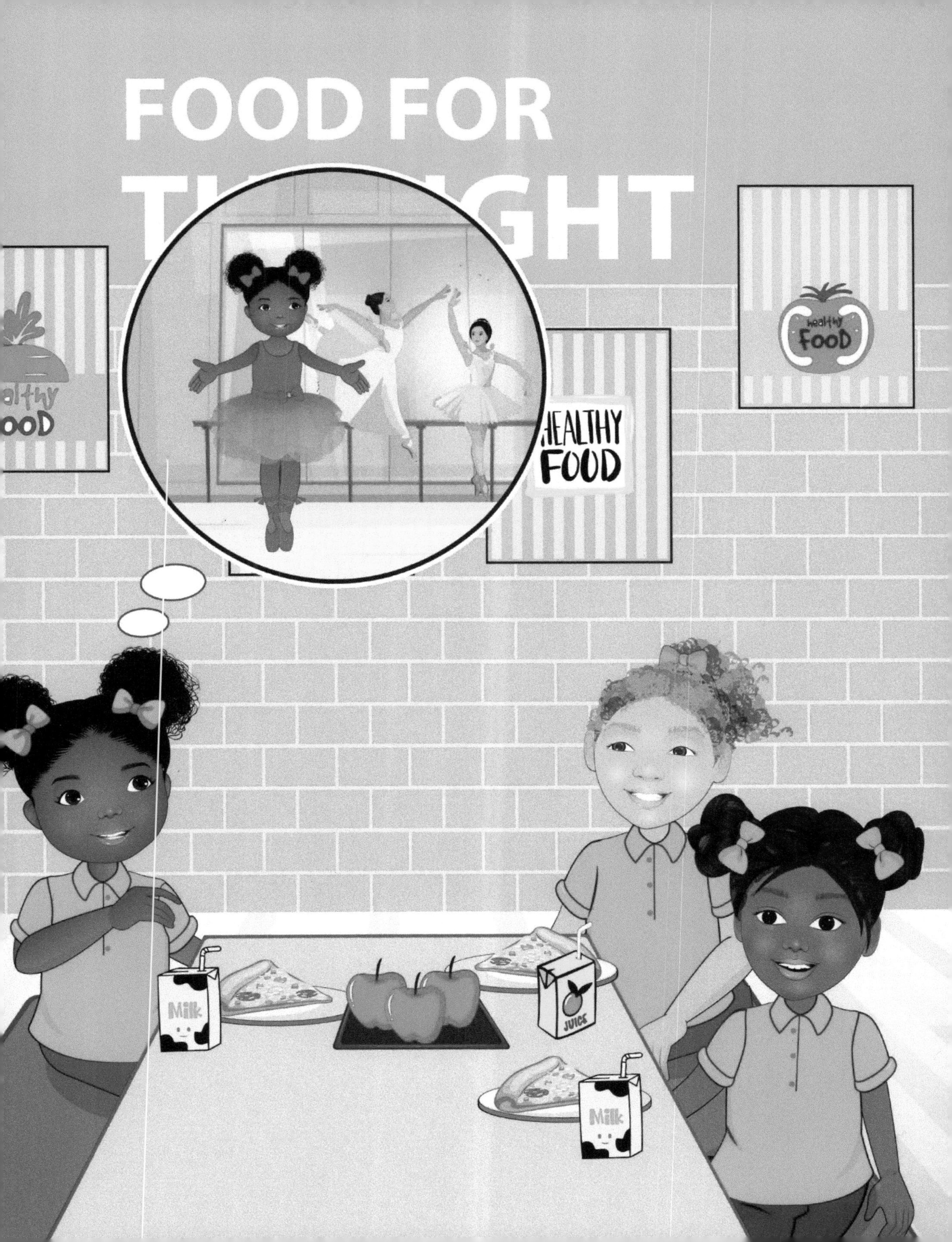
FOOD FOR
healthy
FOOD
HEALTHY
FOOD
Milk
JUICE
Milk

At the end of lunch, the girls walked together to Mrs. Johnson's class. They were all happy and couldn't wait to talk more after school.

At the end of the school day, the girls made a promise that they will never be mean to each other and will always be best friends no matter what!

CPSIA information can be obtained
at www.ICGtesting.com
Printed in the USA
LVHW070034251121
704425LV00005B/93